St. Thomas School Library
West 44th, Mpls.

D1495988

'7 9/08
CLEARANCE
$ 1 00

Chicken Forgets

Chicken Forgets

BY MISKA MILES

ILLUSTRATED BY JIM ARNOSKY

An Atlantic Monthly Press Book

Little, Brown and Company

Boston   Toronto

Books by Miska Miles

Kickapoo	*Apricot ABC*	*Wharf Rat*
Dusty and the Fiddlers	*Annie and the Old One*	*Somebody's Dog*
See a White Horse	*Mississippi Possum*	*Otter in the Cove*
Pony in the Schoolhouse	*Fox and the Fire*	*Gertrude's Pocket*
Teacher's Pet	*Rabbit Garden*	*Tree House Town*
The Pieces of Home	*Nobody's Cat*	*Swim, Little Duck*
Uncle Fonzo's Ford	*Hoagie's Rifle-Gun*	*Chicken Forgets*
	Eddie's Bear	

TEXT COPYRIGHT © 1976 BY MISKA MILES
ILLUSTRATIONS COPYRIGHT © 1976 BY JAMES ARNOSKY

ALL RIGHTS RESERVED. NO PART OF THIS BOOK MAY BE REPRODUCED IN ANY FORM OR BY ANY ELECTRONIC OR MECHANICAL MEANS INCLUDING INFORMATION STORAGE AND RETRIEVAL SYSTEMS WITHOUT PERMISSION IN WRITING FROM THE PUBLISHER, EXCEPT BY A REVIEWER WHO MAY QUOTE BRIEF PASSAGES IN A REVIEW.

Second Printing

T 10/76

Library of Congress Cataloging in Publication Data

Miles, Miska.
    Chicken forgets.

    "An Atlantic Monthly Press book."
    SUMMARY: A forgetful chicken, off to pick black-berries for his mother, almost comes home with flies, weeds, or clover blossoms instead.
    [1. Chickens — Fiction] I. Arnosky, Jim. II. Title.
PZ7.M5944Ch [E]   76-12458
ISBN 0-316-56972-0 lib. bdg.

ATLANTIC-LITTLE, BROWN BOOKS
ARE PUBLISHED BY
LITTLE, BROWN AND COMPANY
IN ASSOCIATION WITH
THE ATLANTIC MONTHLY PRESS

Published simultaneously in Canada
by Little, Brown & Company (Canada) Limited
PRINTED IN THE UNITED STATES OF AMERICA

For Todd and Kevin

Chicken," the mother hen said, "I need your help. I want you to go berry hunting. I need a basket of wild blackberries."

"I'd like to go berry hunting," the little chicken said.

Take this basket and fill it to the top," the mother hen said. "Sometimes you forget things. THIS time, please, please keep your mind on what you are doing. Don't forget."

"I won't forget," the little chicken said. "I'll hunt for wild blackberries."

He started across the meadow. And because he didn't want to forget, he said to himself over and over, "Get wild blackberries. Get wild black-berries."

All the way to the narrow river he kept saying, "Get wild blackberries."

Then the chicken heard the rusty voice of an old frog.

"What are you saying?" the frog asked.

"Get wild blackberries," the chicken said.

"If you're talking to me, you shouldn't say that," the frog said.

"Oh?" said the chicken. "What SHOULD I say?"

"Get a big green fly," the frog said.

The chicken went on his way. And because he didn't want to forget, he said to himself, "Get a big green fly. Get a big green fly."

All the way to the pasture he said, "Get a big green fly."

At the pasture, a goat pushed his head through the rails of the fence and twitched his beard.

"If you are talking to ME," he said, "you should NOT say, 'Get a green fly.' You should say, 'Get green weeds.'"

"Oh?" said the chicken. And on he went, past the pasture, saying, "Get green weeds. Get green weeds."

A bee buzzed over his head.

"What are you mumbling?" the bee asked.

"I was only saying, 'Get weeds,'" the chicken said.

"I think that's wrong," the bee said. "You should say, 'Get clover blossoms.'"

So the little chicken said, "Get clover blossoms."

He said, "Get clover blossoms" all the way to the edge of the cornfield.

"No, no," said a robin. "Berries are better. Follow me."

So the little chicken ran along the ground, following the robin's shadow, and he came to a beautiful patch of wild blackberries.

The robin flew down and ate until he could eat no more.

And the little chicken filled his basket with beautiful, shining wild blackberries.

He started home.

Back he went, through the corn-field and beside the pasture fence by the river.

He ate five berries.

Across the meadow, he went.

And he ate three berries.

At home, the mother hen looked at the basket.

"You DIDN'T forget," she said. "You brought home blackberries, and the basket is almost full."

The little chicken said, "It's easy to remember when you really try."

"I'm proud of you," his mother said.

And the little chicken was proud, too.